A World of Sparkly Princesses

Princess Megerella

does not have tiny feet in glass slippers, or an ugly sister, but she did marry her Prince Charming long long ago and still lives happily ever after. She dreams of turrets, velvety lawns and peacocks, but is quite happy with chimney pots, a back yard and sparrows.

Princess Lulubelle

Princess Lulubelle works in an enchanted studio in a fairytale land full of fun-loving princesses and charming princes. In her spare time she is to be found singing and dancing the night away at palace parties, or tending to her two pet unicorns at the bottom of her garden.

We would like to dedicate this book to two charming and adorable princesses:
Katie and Molly

This edition published in 2009 by
Zero to Ten Limited
Part of the Evans Publishing Group
2A Portman Mansions
Chiltern Street
London
W1U 6NR

First published in 2003 by Zero to Ten Limited.

British Library Cataloguing in Publication Data
A catalogue record for this book
is available from the British Library

ISBN 978 1 84089 542 1

Printed in China on chlorine-free paper
from sustainably maintained forests.

13170400

Contents

What is a princess?   6

What do princesses look like?   8

The bedroom of a princess   10

Becoming a princess   12

Diary of a princess   14

Dating agency   16

Essential life skills   18

Etiquette   19

Princess parties   20

Famous princesses   22

Princess language   23

Princessy things to do   24

Princess in a Temper –   26
the story of an impossible princess

Definition:

A princess is the daughter of a royal family,
or someone who is married to a prince,

But anyone can be a princess if they
feel like one, or behave like one.
So, the world is full of princesses.

What do princesses look like?

Everybody knows what a princess in a fairy story is supposed to look like.

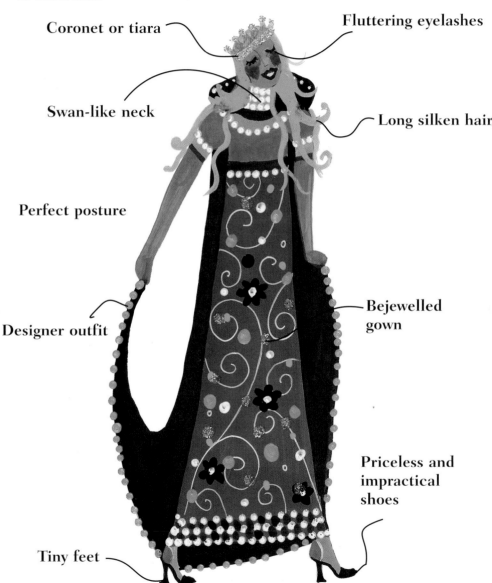

Coronet or tiara

Fluttering eyelashes

Swan-like neck

Long silken hair

Perfect posture

Designer outfit

Bejewelled gown

Priceless and impractical shoes

Tiny feet

However, princesses are often quite ordinary looking
and never have fairy stories written about them.

If you want to be a special princess you can use your
imagination, close your eyes and go into the land of dreams.

The bedroom of a princess

Some princesses are so delicate and sensitive that they can feel the slightest wrinkle in their bed. Every night a lady-in-waiting checks that there are no lumps in the bed or peas* under the mattress, and then smoothes the silken sheets. Modern princesses have duvets and make their own beds, but it is still a good idea to check for peas, crisps and popcorn.

*Read the story of *The Princess and the Pea*

Another servant brushes the princess's hair
a hundred times with a soft brush. Musical instruments
play gently to send her to sleep and the air is filled
with sweet fragrances. Outside her window a nightingale
sings and the princess dreams delightful dreams.
Modern princesses usually brush their own hair
and have a bedtime story to send them to sleep,
but hopefully they still dream happy dreams.

Becoming a princess
a Step-by-Step Guide

1. Overhaul your wardrobe: throw out anything scruffy. Try customising your clothes, and ask the queen (your mother) if you can swap clothes with friends.

2. Eat good, healthy food and drink lots of water. Your complexion will benefit.

3. Dancing is the best exercise for a princess. Walking the royal dogs is good, but riding a unicorn is even better.

4. Remember never to neglect your personal grooming. Princesses always have shiny hair, clean nails and teeth.

5. When speaking, choose your words with care. Never shout or use vulgar language.

6. Think beautiful thoughts. These will show in your face, and you will be a delight to everyone around you.

Of course, you will always make everyone very jealous – but this one of the penalties of being a beautiful princess.

Diary of a princess

Monday:
Had a terrible night. Woke up black-and-blue with bruises from a crumb the chambermaid had left in the bed.

Tuesday:
Awoke early and went to the palace gym for posture practice and dancing lessons. Returned to my bedroom for manicure and hair treatment. Dressed in my silk morning dress and played croquet with the Prince of Tarnia. Declined his marriage proposal.

Wednesday:
Launched a ship.

Thursday:
Attended a medal ceremony for several knights who had rescued damsels in distress. Later, had to be very charming to them all at the state banquet. I think they may wish to marry me. I will decline, of course.

Friday:
Spent all day with my dress designer.
Went to bed early quite exhausted.

Saturday:
Walked in the garden. Rested in the afternoon. This
evening we had a wonderful party in the palace. I wore
some new jewels and my favourite ballgown with the
matching tiara. My dancing went well and everyone was
entranced. Went to bed very late but happy.

Sunday:
Rested.

Dating agency

Of course all the princes,
knights and pirates for miles around
want to marry a wonderful princess,
but princesses have to be very choosy.
There is such a shortage of suitable princes and eligible
bachelors, that an enterprising Fairy Godmother
has started a Royal Dating Agency. Here are
two of the advertisements:

Wanted

Prince for lovely and talented Princess. Must be good-looking and not rough. Must pay constant attention to the Princess and give up horrid hobbies like football and fighting.

I'm afraid I don't match the requirements of this spoilt princess. No thanks.

PRINCE PARAGON

Wanted

Prince for bored Princess. Need not be handsome. Preferably someone with a motorbike who can take her off on adventures. Should be fun-loving and prepared to teach her how to live in the real world.

I must arrange a meeting immediately with this adorable creature. Yes please!

PRINCE PARAGON

Essential life skills

It is most important that princesses are charming
all the time, even if they don't really feel like it.
Here are some examples of charming behaviour:

1. Always greet parents
graciously in the morning.

2. Offer to help others.

3. Be fascinating and interesting at banquets and princess parties.

Etiquette

These are some of the rules of social behaviour which few people bother with today, except princesses.

1. Always wear your crown on formal occasions.

2. Never enter a room after other people – always go first. (Except for trumpeters.)

3. Always be polite to people, otherwise they will think you are snobbish.

4. Only wear trainers with cotton or wool, never with silk or satin.

5. Don't shout.

6. Don't flick peas at mealtimes.

7. Never get angry in pyjamas.

8. Always carry a clean handkerchief – especially if you intend dropping it for a prince to pick up.

Princesses adore giving lavish parties like this one...

1. Grand entrance staircase
2. Banqueting chamber
3. Fizzy drinks fountain
4. Fanfare trumpeters
5. Musical statues

6. Pass the parcel
7. Courtly dancing
8. Court jester
9. Royal gifts

Famous princesses

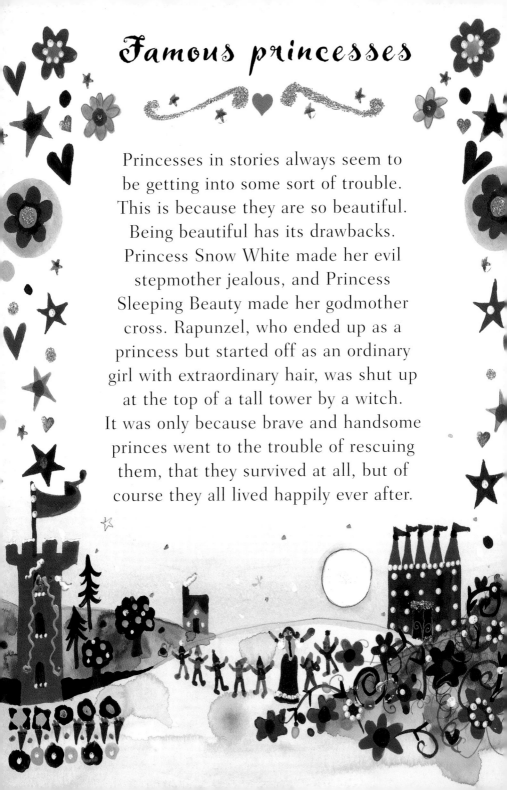

Princesses in stories always seem to be getting into some sort of trouble. This is because they are so beautiful. Being beautiful has its drawbacks. Princess Snow White made her evil stepmother jealous, and Princess Sleeping Beauty made her godmother cross. Rapunzel, who ended up as a princess but started off as an ordinary girl with extraordinary hair, was shut up at the top of a tall tower by a witch. It was only because brave and handsome princes went to the trouble of rescuing them, that they survived at all, but of course they all lived happily ever after.

Princess language

Princesses never use ugly words.
They are taught gracious phrases at Charm School.
Practise these on your friends and family.

'Good morning, dearest mother and father.
Did you sleep well?'

'Sadly, I must decline your gracious
proposal of marriage.'

'Pray accompany me into yonder garden.'

'How sweet of you to risk
your life on my behalf.'

Princessy things to do

Princess Painting

Paint a picture of a fairytale princess
in beautiful gardens. Use lots of
lovely bright colours and add
glitter, stickers and pressed
flowers for finishing touches.

Pressed Flowers

Collect flowers, leaves and grasses.
Spread them out carefully
between sheets of blotting
paper or kitchen roll. Put heavy books
on top until they are dry. Arrange your
pressed flowers on cards or pictures
to give to members of your family,
or your favourite prince . . .

Princess Tea Party

Arrange a party for all your friends,
with special games, drinks and
food, for example
Maids-of-Honour cakes.

Maids-of-Honour Cakes

You will need:
100g ready-made shortcrust pastry
jam
50g sugar
50g self-raising flour
50g butter
1 egg

Directions

Roll out the pastry and
cut circles with a cutter.
Put into a bun tray and
put a spoonful of jam in each.
Make sponge mixture by warming
the butter and mixing it with
the egg, sugar and flour.
Put a spoonful of the
mixture on top of the jam.
Make strips of spare pastry. Place strips
in crosses on top of the cakes.
Bake in a moderate oven for 20 mins.

Princess in a Temper

the story of an impossible princess

T his is the story of Her Royal Highness, Princess Araminta of Sunnyland, and how she became a *real* princess.

She had everything you can imagine to make her happy – kind parents, a beautiful home, a pet unicorn, a bedroom with a silk canopy and murals by Lucy Loveheart, a wardrobe full of designer clothes and a room full of toys. She lived in a fairytale castle with towering turrets and tall walls. Velvety lawns and perfumed gardens were laid out between shady trees and sparkling fountains. Soldiers protected her from danger and servants made her life easy and carefree. Bliss!

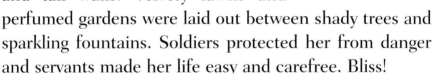

Princess Araminta had skin like apple blossom, long silken hair the colour of honey, eyes as blue as the sky and pearly white teeth with no gaps! Her mother, the queen, called her 'Minty'. Her father, the king, called her 'TROUBLE'. This was because whenever she didn't get her own way, she had the most awful ear-splitting, earth-shaking, terrifying temper tantrums.

Here are some examples:-

Scene 1

ARAMINTA: Pass me my dress.
LADY-IN-WAITING: Here you are, Your Highness.
ARAMINTA: No, silly, I wanted the pink sparkly one by Kevin Clone.

Waaaaaaah!

Scene 2

ARAMINTA: When am I going to Princess Petronilla's pyjama party?
THE QUEEN: Strangely, you weren't invited, Minty.
ARAMINTA: I want to go – I want to go!

Waaaaaaah!

Scene 3

ARAMINTA: Peel me a grape.
MAID: Yes, Your Highness.
ARAMINTA: You've taken off the skin! I wanted to do it myself. I wanted to do it!

Waaaaaaah!

(By the way, did you notice a 'please' or a 'thank you'? No, neither did I.)

One morning at breakfast the King and Queen were talking. They called it a meaningful discussion. The servants called it an argument.

"What are we going to do about Minty? She is becoming quite impossible!"

"It's your fault, my dear; you indulge her far too much!"

"*I* indulge her? That is hardly fair, my love, when you were the one who gave her a diamond-studded laptop for Christmas – only for it to be thrown into the moat because she wanted rubies."

"*You* spoil her."

"*You* just let her get away with everything."

"Excuse me, Your Majesties," said the Lord Chamberlain who was standing by. "I believe that outside the palace gates there are many families who have similar problems with their children and they send them to something called Brat Camp. Oh, I do beg your pardon, I didn't mean to imply that Her Highness is a brat."

"Oh, yes she is!" chorused her parents.

The very next day, Princess Araminta found herself travelling in a golden coach to *The Fairy Godmothers' Charm School*.

What a shock she got! Firstly, her designer clothes had to go and she was given *Fairytrade* organic cotton T-shirts & jogging bottoms. Then she was given a choice for breakfast – eat it or do without. After breakfast, (which she ate), she received her timetable:

9.30 am	Tidy bedroom and clean bathroom
10.00 am	Groom unicorns and muck out stable
11.00 am	Curtseying practice in the hall
12.00 pm	Dancing with Madam Topolova
1.00 pm	Lunch followed by silent reading in the library
2.00 pm	Elocution, voice control and polite conversation
3.00 pm	Etiquette with Princess Megerella
4.00 pm	Tea followed by more silent reading in the library
5.00 pm	Art, music and drama with Lucy Loveheart
6.00 pm	Lecture on discipline by Lord Lofty
7.00 pm	Bed and lights out.

This new regime was astonishing to Araminta! Things got even worse when people started talking back to her in a way she wasn't used to.

Here is a typical conversation with Princess Megerella:

ARAMINTA: What about television?
MEGERELLA: No, sorry.
ARAMINTA: Can I phone my parents?
MEGERELLA: Yes, on Sunday.
ARAMINTA: I want to be sick.
MEGERELLA: Well, you'll have to clear it up yourself.
ARAMINTA: It isn't fair, *Waa...*
MEGERELLA: Don't start that!
ARAMINTA: Will you leave the light on?

MEGERELLA:	You don't need it.
ARAMINTA:	Can I have my teddy?
MEGERELLA:	Yes, if you say please.
ARAMINTA:	Please.
MEGERELLA:	Goodnight, Minty.

Now, all this was the most frightful surprise to poor Araminta. You see, she really thought that because she was a princess she could behave just as she liked. She had never learned that a *real* princess is not the same thing as a *right little* princess! Perhaps you know what I mean? Well, she had to learn the hard way.

It was truly amazing what a healthy diet, a full timetable and firm but fair treatment did for Araminta. If you know of anyone who might benefit from similar treatment, try *The Fairy Godmothers' Charm School* (discount available with this book). Araminta made such good progress that at the end of the week she was sent home.

Her parents were amazed. She was polite, considerate, gracious, charming, grateful and loving – everything, in fact, that a princess should be. Her *Fairytrade* clothes were hung in the wardrobe with her *Kevin Clone* designer dresses, and she even remembered to make her bed in the morning. At last Minty was behaving like a *real* princess. Well, most of the time, that is!